Dear Parent:

Congratulations! Your child is taking the first steps on an exciting journey. The destination? Independent reading!

STEP INTO READING® will help your child get there. The program offers five steps to reading success. Each step includes fun stories and colorful art. There are also Step into Reading Sticker Books, Step into Reading Math Readers, Step into Reading Phonics Readers, Step into Reading Write-In Readers, and Step into Reading Phonics Boxed Sets—a complete literacy program with something for every child.

Learning to Read, Step by Step!

Ready to Read Preschool–Kindergarten
• big type and easy words • rhyme and rhythm • picture clues
For children who know the alphabet and are eager to begin reading.

Reading with Help Preschool–Grade 1
• basic vocabulary • short sentences • simple stories
For children who recognize familiar words and sound out new words with help.

Reading on Your Own Grades 1–3
• engaging characters • easy-to-follow plots • popular topics
For children who are ready to read on their own.

Reading Paragraphs Grades 2–3
• challenging vocabulary • short paragraphs • exciting stories
For newly independent readers who read simple sentences with confidence.

Ready for Chapters Grades 2–4
• chapters • longer paragraphs • full-color art
For children who want to take the plunge into chapter books but still like colorful pictures.

STEP INTO READING® is designed to give every child a successful reading experience. The grade levels are only guides. Children can progress through the steps at their own speed, developing confidence in their reading, no matter what their grade.

Remember, a lifetime love of reading starts with a single step!

For Grant
—J.H.

For Lael and Oliver
—D.G.

Visit us on the Web!
StepIntoReading.com
randomhouse.com/kids

Educators and librarians, for a variety of teaching tools, visit us at
RHTeachersLibrarians.com

Library of Congress Cataloging-in-Publication Data
Holub, Joan.
Dig, scoop, ka-boom! / by Joan Holub ; illustrated by David Gordon.
    p.   cm. — (A step into reading book. Step 1)
Summary: "In rhymed text a group of young friends playing in a sandbox take on the roles of various construction vehicles." — Provided by publisher.
ISBN 978-0-375-86910-5 (trade pbk.) — ISBN 978-0-375-96910-2 (lib. bdg.) — ISBN 978-0-375-98134-0 (ebook)
[1. Stories in rhyme. 2. Construction equipment—Fiction. 3. Play—Fiction.] I. Gordon, David, ill. II. Title.
PZ8.3.H74Dig 2013   [E]—dc23   2012027996

Printed in the United States of America
10 9 8 7 6 5 4 3 2 1

Dig, Scoop, Ka-boom!

by Joan Holub
illustrated by David Gordon

Random House 🏠 New York

Here's the site
and the crew.

They have
a mighty job to do!

Dozer's blade
shapes the land.

Push it. Shove it.
Move that sand!

Digger's teeth
bite the ground.

Crunch, crunch, scoop!
Tracks skid around.

Rocks are big.

They can't stay.

Loader lifts them
all away.

Dump truck comes.
Crash! Ka-boom!

Rocks drop in.

Then off it zooms.

Mixer spins.
Big and strong.

Chugging. Pumping.
All day long.

Crane's tall arm
grabs a beam.

All are working
like a team.

Whistle blows.

Hip-hooray!

Look at what
we built today!

Job's all done.
Play is, too.

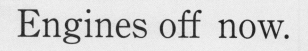

Engines off now.

Good work, crew!